PENGUINAUT!

WRITTEN BY **Marcie Colleen**   ILLUSTRATED BY **Emma Yarlett**

SCHOLASTIC INC.

To Mom and Dad, for being my launch pad. —Marcie

For Isaiah and Solomon, —love Emma

ISBN 978-1-338-32565-2

10 9 8 7 6 5 4 3 2 1   18 19 20 21 22

Printed in the U.S.A.   169
First printing 2018

The text type was set in Warnock Pro Bold.
The title type was hand-lettered by Emma Yarlett.
The illustrations were done in watercolor, collage, pencil, crayon, pen, and paint.
Book art direction and design by Marijka Kostiw

Orville was small.

His friends were BIG.

And their
adventures
were BIGGER.

Orville longed for *big* adventures, too.

One day, he announced his plans for the **biggest**

and best adventure yet.

Orville flippered out.

He tried to flap — KERPLOP!

KERPLOP

He tried to climb — WHACK!

He tried to catapult — fa-LING!

OUCH!

. . . and landed in the reptile house.
Orville was pretty sure the
boa constrictor was not trying to hug him.

Still Orville kept trying.

He borrowed from
the zookeeper.
He nicked from
the trash cans.
He built and built.

DO
NOT
BEND

And with

a shake,

shake,

shake

of a half-filled

soda bottle,

the ship

was

ready

for

liftoff.

It was perfect.

And perfectly

penguin-sized.

With a trembling flipper salute,

he took his place at the controls.

BLAST-
OFF!

WHOOSH!

The ship zipped through the night sky,

through clouds, over stars,

and straight to the moon.

BUMP

KERPLUMP

KABOOM!

Orville landed.

His stomach
felt queasy.
His spacesuit
felt squeezy.
Now that
he'd made it,
what would
he do?

He took a small step.

He hopped.

Did a little dance.

And tripped.

TUMBLE BUMBLE

He somersaulted with stars,

cartwheeled over craters,

BA
BOING!

and giggled for all the galaxy to hear.

It was the BIGGEST and best adventure yet.

"I'm doing it myself!" he cheered,

but his tiny voice was swallowed up

in the starry blackness.

Orville stopped.

He was all alone.

His stomach grew queasier.

His spacesuit grew squeezier.

He shivered

and a note fell out

of his pocket.

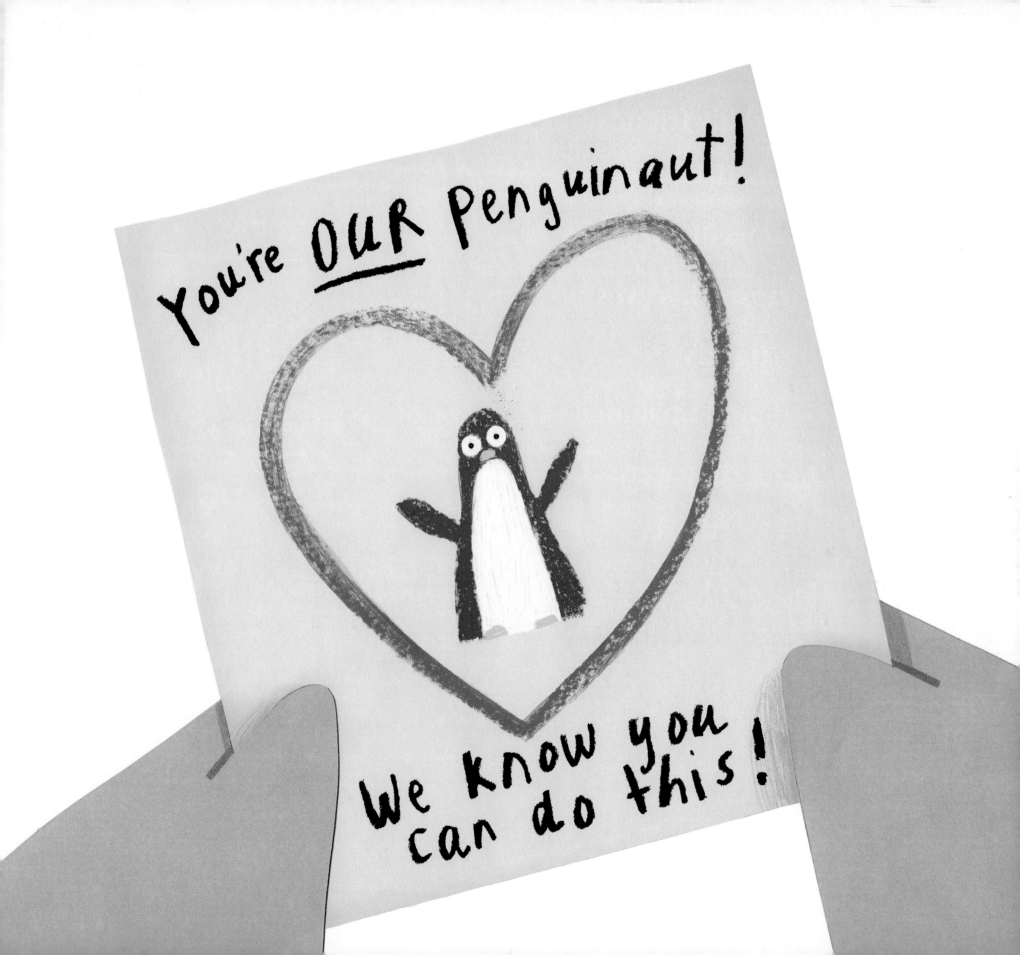

He missed his friends.

So Orville

closed his eyes

tightly

and imagined

they were

there.

When he was safely back in his ship,

he looked toward home.

He couldn't wait to tell everyone

about his **big** adventure.

Sure, Orville's friends

were BIG.

Now the proud Penguinaut

felt BIG, too.

ELEPHANTS

Orville

But BIGGEST of all?

Being together
was out
of this world.

3, 2, 1 . . .

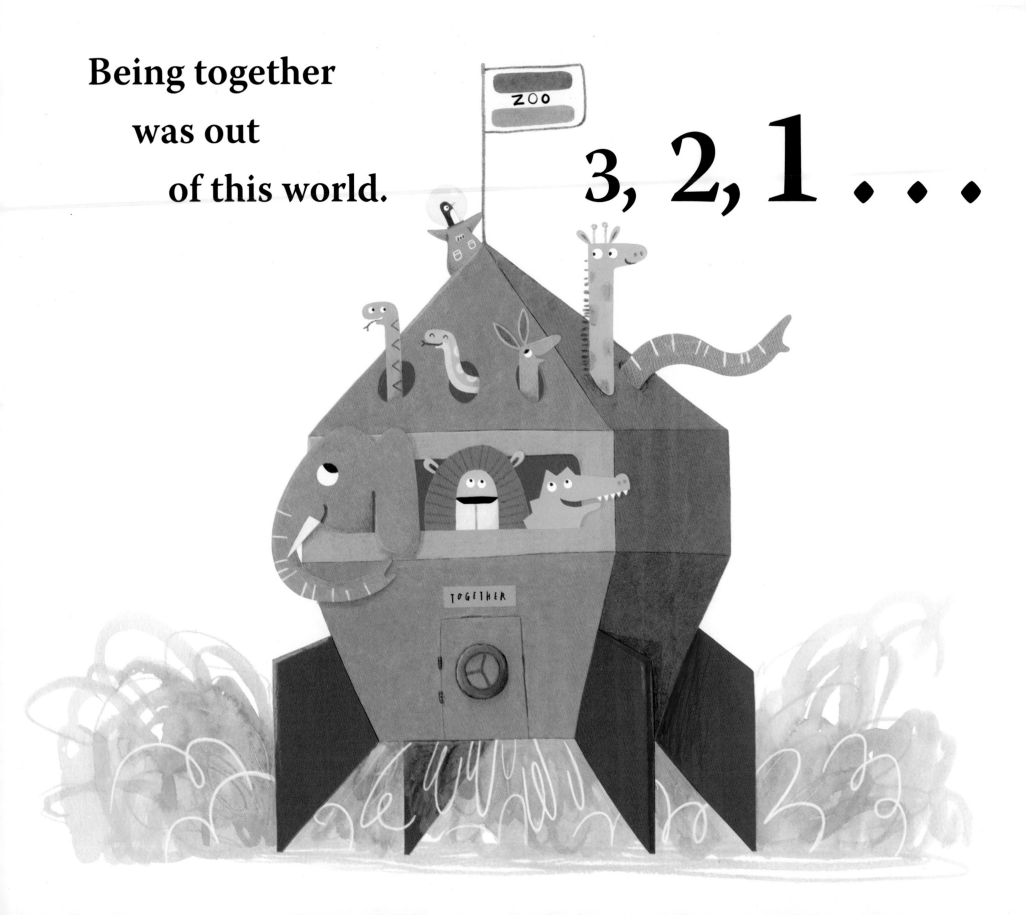